Peculiar Pets

Poems From The UK

Edited By Allie Jones

First published in Great Britain in 2021 by:

Young Writers
Remus House
Coltsfoot Drive
Peterborough
PE2 9BF
Telephone: 01733 890066
Website: www.youngwriters.co.uk

All Rights Reserved
Book Design by Ashley Janson
© Copyright Contributors 2020
Softback ISBN 978-1-80015-141-3

Printed and bound in the UK by BookPrintingUK
Website: www.bookprintinguk.com
YB0454D

★ FOREWORD ★

Welcome Reader!

Are you ready to discover weird and wonderful creatures that you'd never even dreamed of?

For Young Writers' latest competition we asked primary school pupils to create a Peculiar Pet of their own invention, and then write a poem about it! They rose to the challenge magnificently and the result is this fantastic collection full of creepy critters and amazing animals!

Here at Young Writers our aim is to encourage creativity in children and to inspire a love of the written word, so it's great to get such an amazing response, with some absolutely fantastic poems. Not only have these young authors created imaginative and inventive animals, they've also crafted wonderful poems to showcase their creations and their writing ability. These poems are brimming with inspiration. The slimiest slitherers, the creepiest crawlers and furriest friends are all brought to life in these pages – you can decide for yourself which ones you'd like as a pet!

I'd like to congratulate all the young authors in this anthology, I hope this inspires them to continue with their creative writing.

CONTENTS

Al Khair Primary School, Oldbury

Alizah Khattak (9)	1
Zikra Maryam (9)	2
Kaysan Burrell (10)	4
Yasir Yusuf (11)	5
Abubakr Tousef (9)	6
Rumaysa Inaya Muskaan Farooq (10)	7

Codsall Middle School, Codsall

Eleanor Birch (9)	8
Chloe Lloyd (9)	10
Angel Johnson (9)	11
Keira Beddows (9)	12
Demi Younger (9)	14
Emily Walters (9)	16
Amy Lacey (9)	17
Carlie McLelland (9)	18
Mark Filimonov (9)	19
Erika Steventon (9)	20
Lexi Spittle (9)	21
Olivia Davies (9)	22
Kiki Guest (9)	23
Maddison Orlowski (9)	24
Izzy Hetherington (10)	26
Moira Alawneh (9)	27
Max Lyne-Greybanks (9)	28
Beatrix Shephard (9)	29
Joshua Wise (9)	30
Ellouise Brant (9)	31
Euan Robb (9)	32
Alice Cattell (9)	33
George Roalfe (9)	34
Kayla Whitehouse (9)	35
Lea Plimmer (9)	36
Maisie Younger (9)	37
Sienna Rogers (10)	38
Jack Rhodes (9)	39
Oliver Gittens (10)	40
Edward Riley (10)	41
Harri Cartwright (9)	42
Harry Ness (9)	43
Ruben Patel (10)	44
Ella Ridgway (9)	45
Noah Hydon	46
Esme Talbot (9)	47
Chloe Richards (10)	48
Tristan Moore (10)	49
Amy Thompson	50
Emilia Wiggin	51
Chloe Elliman (10)	52
Jasper Lowe (9)	53
Jessica Simmonds (10)	54
Willow Roalfe	55
Brooke Platt (10)	56
Jacob Holden (10)	57
Ben Robinson (9)	58
Aarian Gill (9)	59
Lola Gillen (10)	60
Danniella Shore (10)	61
Safa Qasim (9)	62
Lola Jackson	63
Isaac Danbury (9)	64
Rosie Sayers (9)	65
Reginald Myers (10)	66
Jacob Rhead (10)	67
Felix Davis (9)	68
Sam Akers (9)	69
Avni Chodha (9)	70

JJ Garbett	71
Ella-Mae Thompson-Wiggin (9)	72
Reuben Price (9)	73
Austin Winwood (10)	74
Bronny Lloyd	75
Liam Lewis (9)	76
Charlie Deaville (9)	77
Amelia Hotchkiss (9)	78
Harry Dornan (10)	79
Arjan Bassi (9)	80

Elmwood School, Walsall

Jack Poxon (11)	81
Carson Price (12)	82
Cody Love-Knight	83
Francis Gosling	84
Logan Hawley (11)	85
Tyler-Reece Jones (11)	86
Sennen Gregory (11)	87
Dilan Smith (11)	88

Halfway Primary School, Llanelli

Seren Pantall (10)	89
Annabelle O'Neill (9)	90
Maia Jones (9)	91
Fern Prescott (9)	92
Olivia Lewis	93
Harri Howells	94
Megan Lemon (9)	95
Ollie Grant (9)	96
Rocco Thomas (10)	97
Riley Hanley (10)	98

Krishna Avanti Primary School, Evington

Priyanka Kala (8)	99
Payal Keshvala (8)	100
Anaya Kishori Dasi (9)	102
Leah Mapara (8)	104
Elissia Dharamshi (8)	106
Riaa Kotecha (11)	107
Esha Modha (8)	108
Khushi Parekh	109
Alisha Mistry (10)	110
Riya Mandalia (8)	111
Diya B Modhwadia (8)	112
Vivaan Jhala (7)	113
Aarya Patel (9)	114
Pavitra Patel (9)	115
Dilan Chauhan (9)	116
Mitali Patel (8)	117
Siya Anadkat (7)	118
Ansh Shah (9)	119
Khunti (8)	120
Bhavani Nayee (10)	121
Anya Sawjani (9)	122
Divya Chauhan (10)	123
Nihal Jitesh Patel (8)	124
Dhruvi Sani (7)	125
Shania Desai (8)	126
Dhriti Lakhani (10)	127
Rahul Nathwani (9)	128
Isha Soni (10)	129
Nevaan Lakhani (7)	130
Aaryan Bapodra (9)	131
Shruti Karelia (8)	132
Niya Patel (8)	133
Jhanvi Vyas (8)	134
Pia Mistry (10)	135
Anya Kotecha (7)	136
Yogiraj Dixit (9)	137
Harini Vinothkumar (9)	138
Keshavi Naker (8)	139
Devraj Nayee (8)	140
Ayanna Kotecha (7)	141
Disha Ranpura (9)	142
Neeva Shah (8)	143
Nandakishore Mundalappa (8)	144
Shriya Solanki (8)	145
Shivam Mistry (8)	146
Aditya Madhwani (7)	147
Hashini Vinoth Kumar (9)	148
Kush Popat (8)	149
Anay Mistry (9)	150

Neha Bharakhada (8)	151
Kalindi Priya Carrillo (9)	152
Avi Patel (8)	153
Shanaya Kotecha (10)	154
Keya Joshi (8)	155
Cherry-Mae Kotecha (8)	156
Tanish Patel (8)	157
Heerav Chudasama (8)	158
Mahi Parmar (8)	159
Janvi Khunti (10)	160
Anaya Ramaiya (7)	161
Dilan Rana (9)	162
Heer Jethwa (8)	163
Riya Mistry	164

Partney CE (A) Primary School, Partney

Enzo Lanzetta (10)	165
Oscar Morris (10)	166
Fraiser Lyall (10)	168
Lois Louth (9)	170
Abigail Sands (11)	171
Peter Gates (10)	172
Ethan Turner (10)	173
Phoebe Lennon (10)	174
Lilli Edwards (10)	175
Marley Biney	176
Toby Sutton (10)	177
Oscar Warren (10)	178
Adam Middleton (10)	179
Gracie Stroud (10)	180

St Mary's Catholic Primary School, Little Crosby

Harriet Jones (9)	181
Molly Tarpey (10)	182
Elsie Croxton (9)	183
Stevie-Leigh Connaughton (10)	184
Grace Hayes (9)	185
Lucy Bovill (9)	186
Liam Yates (10)	188
Eleanor Arthur	189

Caleb Still (10)	190
Nathan Hughes	192
Margot Buckley (10)	193
Zoe Hill (9)	194
Isabella Williams (9)	195
Lauren Clegg (9)	196
Angel-Rose Banner (10)	197
Angelica Moffett (10)	198
Emily West (10)	199
Callum Clegg (10)	200
Matthew Cunliffe-Davies (9)	201
Lucy Bromilow (10)	202
Summer Aldridge (10)	203

St Pius X Catholic Preparatory School, Fulwood

Fahd Patel (10)	204
Abdullah Hussein (9)	206
Aamina Ali (9)	207
Beatrice Constable (8)	208
Aayush Patel (8)	209
Faheem Patel (8)	210
Gerard Ologbosere (8)	211
Hashim Syed Shoab	212
Zain Ahmad (9)	213
Keean Taherian (9)	214
Sophie Fitzherbert (9)	215
Amelia Kovvuri (9)	216

THE POEMS

Incredible Blue Badge

I ncredible Blue Badge is as
N eat as a bookshelf
C olourful and creative
R eally an artist
E ager to make friends
D azzling like the galaxy
I ncredible portals he makes
B lazing sprinting shoes
L ovely tea he makes
E xtraordinary books he writes

B lue Badge is
L ucky like the stars
U cky is his bedroom
E arth is his new home

B lue is his favourite colour
A mazing are the cakes he makes
D ashing are his looks
G entle as a feather
E xcellent is the real Blue Badge!

Alizah Khattak (9)
Al Khair Primary School, Oldbury

The Fat, Furry, Flimsy, Ferocious Feline

There was once a guy called Bigums
He was a great furry cat and always begged from mums
They would give him chicken or dead lambs and even fish and frogs

Sometimes he would steal food
Wink and smile like a dude
Got so big, he crushed the town
And people were in a very bad mood

People got annoyed at his furry mess
Even the posh, prim cat Tess
People agreed that he was tameless
Some would say that he was full of wildness

His T-shirt ripped and his eyes turned sore
But he'd still eat food, more and more
He'd carry on begging from door to door

Bigums and Tess were from the same mum
So was the ginger, gruesome, grumpy cat Tom
Bigums was once one stone, now was 101 tons!

People made a plan, a very marvellous plan
They told every single man
To get the smelliest hugest lamb

They lured him with lamb with big fat grins
Little did Bigums know there was a shiny pin
They popped him so he hadn't a single sin

So beware of the fat, furry, flimsy, ferocious feline!

Zikra Maryam (9)
Al Khair Primary School, Oldbury

The Couch Potato!

Who is this adorable rat
With fangs so big they scare off the bats?

It has purple fur and jet-black eyes
He might scare you at first but he is nothing to despise

The small creature doesn't stay in bed in the winter
And when it comes to cheesy garlic bread, he's a bit of a sprinter

He breathes ice and fire too
If you hurt him he'll fire at you

When you give him broccoli he thinks, no!
But when he has nachos he's a couch potato

He can read your mind with his green antennas
And when he does I tell him that's bad manners!

Kaysan Burrell (10)
Al Khair Primary School, Oldbury

_a The Frontflipper

_a is a gorgeous shade of pink
_ly and kind, but she's a very peculiar pet
_ of her hobbies is tumbling
_ery day she flips out of bed!
_oving her splits
_eaping from one side of her room to the other
_nd then gliding down the stairs

T he tricks she does are super hard
H er hoop hangs from the ceiling
E very morning she sits in her hoop

F eathery tufts of pink
R acing down the garden
O nto the bars
N ever falling off!
T hen jumping off perfectly

My Dragon

A purple, pale dragon
Which looks like a mess

Even if washed
He still stinks like a bin

If you try to take my pet
Then good luck to you

He will burn you down
With his fire-breathing breath

Even if he looks like a good pet
Touch him and you will regret

He's super cute when he sits on my lap
But when he's hungry he acts like a bat

When I'm hungry he bakes me cookies
And puts on some tea too

And when I'm done
He'll get my slippers for me.

Yasir Yusuf (11)
Al Khair Primary School, Oldbury

Brilliant Bird

He soars high in the sky watching your daily life,
When he is low, he likes to pound the ground,
What a brilliant bird!

He is agile, he is ferocious,
He is clever and he is cunning,
What a brilliant bird!

His claws grip the wall,
He is feathery, he is strong,
What a brilliant bird!

He has a razor-sharp beak, he is vicious,
He is colourful, he is marvellous,
What a brilliant bird!

Abubakr Tousef (9)
Al Khair Primary School, Oldbury

Aby The Artist

A by is the greatest gorilla
   artistic gorilla
B eing the best gorilla in the
Y anking the paint on the board
   artistic drawing

T omorrow she's going to sell her
   picture
H opefully all of the people will love the
E xcitedly Aby ran around the house finishing
   her paintings

A by went to sleep ready for the big day
   tomorrow
R ight away Aby woke in the morning and ate her
   breakfast
T oday, Aby heard a knock on the door
I t was the government asking for the painting
S he said, "Sure, that will be £5," but the
   government gave Aby extra
T he government gave Aby £500, she was so
   happy!

Angel Johnson (9)
Codsall Middle School, Codsall

F lapping her wings with glee
L iving the dream
I love my flamingo
P erfect and cute
P eculiar but amazing
E xtraordinary and talented
R ound of applause!

Keira Beddows (9)
Codsall Middle School, Codsall

Max The Bossy Traffic Warden

M aking everyone pay
A lways hardworking
X -ray vision, he can see through walls to find poor parkers

T raffic is always hard for him
H elping out people who don't know where to park
E xpert polar bear warden

T ells people off
R unning to the next problem
A ware
F rustrating
F antastic at making sure that everybody has parked well
I nteresting things happen when he is patrolling
C ar crashes nearly every day

W arning people constantly
A ll around the city there are accidents with cars
R unning from place to place
D oesn't let you park for free
E ncouraging people to pay
N ever happy!

Demi Younger
Codsall Middle School, Codsall

Charlie Camouflage

C amouflage is my favourite thing
H ow happy it makes me feel
A mazing animals, I can do them all
R abbits, dogs and a lot more
L ittle ones, big ones, thin and fat
I magine how it makes me feel
E xcellent elephants are my favourite ones to turn into

C harlie is my name, Charlie the camo cat!
A ny animal, no problem at all
M ost people think I'm an ordinary cat
O nly me and you know the truth
U nless I become famous
F olks will never know the truth
L ook, listen, I'm so clever
A nd this must remain our secret
G ot to go now - think I'm needed
E lephant gone missing, help wanted!

Emily Walters (9)
Codsall Middle School, Codsall

Loki The Climbing Dog

L oving Loki is a great climber
O n a wall all the time
K eeps looking for something higher
I nside doing rock climbing

T remendous climbing
H igher, higher he will go
E ven to the top of a skyscraper

C an you climb as high as Loki?
L oki is the best climber
I wish I could climb as high as Loki
M ight he fall if he doesn't take care?
B ecause the buildings are so tall
I t is scary to watch
N ever going to fall
G ot to concentrate so hard

D ogs are not really good climbers
O nce he reaches the very top
G lad he made it - now just the slide down!

Amy Lacey (9)
Codsall Middle School, Codsall

Max The Spy Agent

M ax is a very secretive starfish
A stonishing Max the starfish loves to act astonishing
X -ray vision, Max loves to use X-ray vision all the time

T umbles, Max tumbles like cats
H elpful, Max loves to be helpful
E normous, he does humungous flips

S neaky, Max loves to be sneaky all the time
P atrolling, Max goes patrolling most of the time
Y ellow, Max loves the colour yellow

A stonishing, he loves the word astonishing
G round, that's where he spies
E vil, he can be really evil sometimes
N ew scooter, Max gets a new scooter every time he spies
T rouble, Max is always causing trouble!

Carlie McLelland (9)
Codsall Middle School, Codsall

Rocket Ride The Cycler

R ide is my peculiar pet
O ctopus is his occupation
C ycling is what he's best at
K ind and generous
E njoying every time he rides
T ired or not, he always goes on

R ide is as quick as a rocket
I ncredibly fast
D rums he's fabulous at playing
E xpert at cycling

T he octopus is very talented
H e's got eight tentacles
E legantly swims

C ycling is what he normally does
Y ellow or orange, what's his colour?
C ycling everywhere, he never stops
L ong tentacles are very useful
E ven tentacles
R acing, he always wins.

Mark Filimonov (9)
Codsall Middle School, Codsall

Lamacorn And Me

I found him when I was seven
Walking past the shop
I felt his magic gaze which made me stop
It's like it was meant to be
My lamacorn and me.

I took him home and gave him love
And then whoosh!
He expanded his wings to make him fly
I jumped on his back and we flew to the sky
It's good to be free
My lamacorn and me.

He's my bestie forever
He's gentle, loving and clever
His bright, multicoloured, soft, fluffy fur
Is as soft as a cloud on a warm summer day
His golden horn shines as bright as a star in the night sky
It was like it was meant to be
My lamacorn and me.

Erika Steventon (9)
Codsall Middle School, Codsall

The Fancy Mousie Doggy Swimming Doggo

One day I adopted a dog called The Fancy Mousie Doggy Swimming Doggo
That morning I woke up and last night he slept behind the TV!
He crawled slyly from behind the TV
And I carefully poured dog food into his sparkly bowl
He rushed into the kitchen and gobbled up all the spoons!
Soon after he pooped strawberry laces that smelt like fish!
I went outside and blew up a mini pool
An hour later he jumped out and shook his neon, glittery fur
Then he hugged me softly while I watched TV
Then he curled back up in his soft, comfy bed
I noticed he's no normal pet...
And that's why he's special to me!

Lexi Spittle (9)
Codsall Middle School, Codsall

Astonishing Ally

A lly is a very peculiar pet
S he is not just a starfish
T he starfish is an astronaut
O h Ally, she's amazing!
N eptune, she's been to them all
I ndependent, she is independent
S he's astonishing
H ungry, every time she goes to space she's hungry
I ndependent as I said, she does everything on her own
N eptune was her favourite
G ames, she loves to play games in space as well

A stonishing, she's amazing
L eaps into the air
L oves jumping planet to planet
Y ahooo!

Olivia Davies (9)
Codsall Middle School, Codsall

Merpug The First

My merpug is as tiny as can be
He can change into a rat or anything you say
We were going for a walk high in the say
He changed into a dog then he was gone
His staff helps him fly high in the sky
He is such a good merpug, even better than me
My merpug is clever, he is in the sky
He eats frogs' legs and pug legs the same
Time to meet new friends
If you are mean, you are his tea, hee hee!
He likes changing into a pug tall and small
But it's not his favourite after all
His favourite is changing like a worm long and slimy
All day long!

Kiki Guest (9)
Codsall Middle School, Codsall

Super Spy Sausage Sammy

S uper spy, Sammy Sausage
U seful plans he has
P erfect sausage shape
E pic disguises like fake moustaches
R eally fast change

S neaky trips
P erfect plans
Y ummy flavour

S uper service
A mazing ideas
U nbelievable timing
S mart thinking
A dorable spy
G reat work
E xtraordinary

S pecialist
A wesome times
M agnificent hiding
M agic transformation
Y es to Sammy!

Maddison Orlowski (9)
Codsall Middle School, Codsall

Narpugunicorn

N ever as cute
A Narpuguni swims in the sea
R iding with her is me!
P repare for an adventure with Narpuguni
U nite with other creatures like her
G reat when swimming in the sea
U nite these creatures, please, please!
N ot for sale, she's mine forever
I sn't she so cute?
C aring and kind she will be forever
O n her own it's no help to the world
R ight next to me is where she should be
N ever a fairy tale, it's real, it's real!

Izzy Hetherington (10)
Codsall Middle School, Codsall

The Weirdest Snake On Earth

I was creeping through the jungle one day,
When I saw it there plain as day,
It was hanging from a tree,
Right in front of me,
Body bright yellow,
With black stripes soft as mellow,
With rainbow wings,
Such beautiful things,
With a shark fin tail,
I touched it, rough as mail,
I saw the spider legs
They were as sharp as pegs,
I looked at the fangs,
They made my heart pang!
Those fangs could pack a powerful punch,
I only saw it once,
It slithered back up the tree,
Like it was meant to be.

Moira Alawneh (9)
Codsall Middle School, Codsall

Harley The Hotwash

I took my dog to work
Harley gives the hottest car washes
Always hardworking
And persevering
Careful, elegant washer
And *whoosh!*
In a flash he is washing the car
He is the best at car washing ever!
He wags his tail to wipe the car clean
How good do you think he is?
How much do you think he will get paid today?
A lot!
The way he washes the cars with his furry behind is unique
You won't get this wash anywhere else
It's an experience you won't forget!

Max Lyne-Greybanks (9)
Codsall Middle School, Codsall

Edmund The Extinguished

Edmund dashed to the rescue
The fire crackled and popped
Crack, pop, crackle
He could hear a scream
He sucked up the contents of the bucket
Splash, splash, splash
A jet of water came out his trunk
He extinguished the flames
Red, orange, yellow
His high-vis jacket shone brightly
Edmund stomped into the building
Splish, splash, splosh
Another jet of water came out his natural hose
The fire was fully extinguished
Edmund jumped for joy!

Beatrix Shephard (9)
Codsall Middle School, Codsall

Magical Mr Tips

M ind-blowing superhero
A wesome at flying
G entle and kind
I ntelligent tracking down enemies
C ourageous and never scared
A dorable but has razor-sharp claws
L egendary ninja skills

M agnificent at being sneaky and quiet
R oars like a lion

T iny brave cat
I ncredible at being sneaky
P eckish all the time
S mart and always outwits criminals.

Joshua Wise (9)
Codsall Middle School, Codsall

Jimmy The Giraffe

Jimmy the giraffe likes a good laugh
He lives at the zoo, close to Miss Kangaroo
Jimmy the giraffe has lots of sass
He likes to pose for photographs
Jimmy the giraffe likes a good laugh
He loves to have a bubble bath

Jimmy the giraffe makes me laugh
He stands so high with his head in the sky
He is brown, yellow and red
With two funny bumps on top of his head
Jimmy the giraffe likes a good laugh
I love you Jimmy the giraffe!

Ellouise Brant (9)
Codsall Middle School, Codsall

Euan's Gion

Gordon the Gion
He eats like a lion
But sleeps like a humble giraffe.

He is cool but friendly
And still makes everyone laugh.

His top speed is quick
And he's cunning and slick
He'll be gone by the time you say, "Hi,"
Vroom, whoosh!

His legs are stilts
Towering high in the sky
His head is a baby's face
He thinks he's cool and to be true
Everyone thinks he's ace!

Euan Robb (9)
Codsall Middle School, Codsall

Mega Turtle

M ega Turtle has a tiny head
E nchanting shell shines all night
G iant shell, you can ride on it
A mazing rainbow shell changes colours

T o the rescue she comes, get ready to be amazed!
U p and down she swims across the ocean
R apidly she changes colours every day
T o red, green and orange
L oving, caring, all there can be
E xcellent she is, well done Mega Turtle!

Alice Cattell (9)
Codsall Middle School, Codsall

Pacoon

He lived in a lagoon,
He often went to the saloon,
The pacoon sat in a tree,
Just the pacoon and me.
But at 8am,
The sushi shop went into mayhem,
When Pacoon got to his job,
He started to serve the angry mob.
He got a sushi roll,
And put it in a bowl.
Pacoon had a friend,
Sometimes his friend drove him round the bend!
His friend was Dat,
Dat slept on a mat,
And Pacoon liked that.

George Roalfe (9)
Codsall Middle School, Codsall

Indigo The Invisible!

Indigo is me
I'm a very special dog
I can go invisible and camouflage
I do this to listen to Boris Johnson
And his very evil plans!
I have to wear disguises
Dresses, beard, glasses and moustaches
Big Boris is planning that cute animals should go to their own world
Crazy, silly words like
Oranges, pineapple, watermelon, turn me invisible
I'm such a cute dog
I tell myself that anyway!

Kayla Whitehouse (9)
Codsall Middle School, Codsall

Duck Dog!

Walking on the ceiling as it barks in the graveyard where it digs
Playing with the bones leftover from its meal
Dark blue body and glow-in-the-dark yellow eyes
Orange patches all over its body
Blood-red lasers it shoots from its million eyes
It sleeps in a ripped double bed
In the night it plays in the graveyard and hangs around funerals
It is the size of a large pig
And it gives everyone the shivers!

Lea Plimmer (9)
Codsall Middle School, Codsall

My Fairy Merdog

Every time she gets home,
She starts to howl and growl.

When I get up,
My Merdog gets up, woofing happily.

She is a sleepy, lazy dog,
That sleeps all day.

Today she jumped on my lap,
When she was scared.

Then walked away when it was dark,
And very black.

When she went for a walk,
She saw lots of rainbow laces,
And they tasted like cola laces!

Maisie Younger (9)
Codsall Middle School, Codsall

Gurtrude The Giraffe

G orgeous giraffe, purple and blue
U nbelievable talent in make-up, just like you
R ed glowing lipstick which glows in the dark
T ons of make-up, but loads of eyes
R unning in the park is her favourite thing to do
U nusual sense of taste because she eats Skittles
D elicate in her movement, so calm and beautiful
E xcellent talents and excellent pet!

Sienna Rogers (10)
Codsall Middle School, Codsall

Racket Ralph

R alph loves to play tennis
A n amazing expert athlete
C atches the ball every single time
K eeps playing non-stop
E xpert dog player, is fast
T remendous serves

R acket Ralph never stops
A lways moving
L ooking left and right
P assing the ball to the other side
H itting the ball as fast as he can.

Jack Rhodes (9)
Codsall Middle School, Codsall

The Rainsupercorn

R ainbow farts and fur
A mazingly fluffy and cute
I ncredibly colourful
N asty sometimes, but for a reason
S oft and cuddly
U nicorn as a superhero!
P owers are farting rainbows and can fly
E xcitement for a cuddle
R eally naughty
C ute like a puppy
O utstanding
R eally cute
N oisy!

Oliver Gittens (10)
Codsall Middle School, Codsall

Vinnie 1000

V innie 1000 is a special pet
I t is a robot dog!
N ight-time is his favourite time to play
N ormally he likes to perform fire shows
I n the day he eats and sleeps
E very year he plays along

1 ,000 pounds is his price
0 days he will not want to play
0 times he poops inside
0 chance he will not love you.

Edward Riley (10)
Codsall Middle School, Codsall

Raj The Rockin' Racoon

This is a poem about a racoon
That rocks and rocks until his socks blow off!

The racoon can sometimes be crazy
A lot of the time he is very lazy

He can play an awesome guitar
And because of that he has a very posh car!

The racoon is so loud
It can sometimes make you frown

Because the racoon is so rich
It sometimes can attract a witch!

Harri Cartwright (9)
Codsall Middle School, Codsall

Patric Star

P utting on epic disguises like a dress
A lways sticking to windows
T rying to find secret facts
R eally easy to spy on people
I t's time to roll out, yeah!
C onstantly sticking to windows

S tarting to stick
T remble over the mouldy patio
A nd it's so easy to spy
R olling into the house.

Harry Ness (9)
Codsall Middle School, Codsall

King Superhero

The dog lives in a house, it is way bigger than a mouse,
He is the king that's why he wears a ring,
He is super cool, he loves to go in the pool,
He loves dairy, that's why he is very hairy,
He has got a beard, that's why he is very weird,
He loves mustard, he even likes custard,
He wears a crown that's dark brown,
He loves poo, he even lives on the loo!

Ruben Patel (10)
Codsall Middle School, Codsall

Lioncat

I adopted a cat,
When I got home she lay on the mat,
And then she found a rat,
Then she lay on the mat again,
At 2am I heard a bang,
It wasn't now just a cat,
It was a lioncat with wings!
I sat with lioncat on the sofa,
She lifted up,
She found a pup,
I took the pup and the cat,
And they lay on the mat,
Then they fell asleep.

Ella Ridgway (9)
Codsall Middle School, Codsall

Billy The Fish

B illy is black as coal, with smooth scales and blue eyes like the midnight sky
I like to watch him swim around and wonder what he is thinking of
L iving in a fish tank is no problem for Billy because he is a teleporting fish
L ong ago, Billy teleported into a tropical fish tank but he got hot
Y ouch! Too hot. So he teleported back home!

Noah Hydon
Codsall Middle School, Codsall

Rooney And The Nits

Rooney likes to walk in the park,
He likes to go outside,
Until he got nits,
Now they get a free ride!
We took him to the vets
And all they would say,
Is, "I'm sorry ma'am,
But they will have to stay."
He loves his meat and biscuits
But what about the nits?
We had to get more dogs,
So I buy the meats and bits!

Esme Talbot (9)
Codsall Middle School, Codsall

Super Star!

S uper Star can fly so high!
U p and up in the sky,
P erfect powers,
E xcellent, clever and incredible,
R ainbow supersuit with every colour.

S tars bow down to her in the dark,
T errific powers, so so cool,
A dorable and as cute as a baby kitten,
R espectable, playful and cool!

Chloe Richards (10)
Codsall Middle School, Codsall

Cyber Crab

C yber Crab is a special pet
Y et he moves just like a human
B ut he's still a little crab!
E verything he does is sideways
R eally smart at everything

C omputers are his favourite toy
R ushes through all his work
A lways first to finish though
B ut eager to start all over.

Tristan Moore (10)
Codsall Middle School, Codsall

Thing

There's a flamingo mixed with a horse
It is very peculiar
It has a brown, hairy, knotty tail
What a peculiar pet
It has a flamingo's head with a hairy mane
It is as big as 50 double-decker buses
It has a baby called Sam
He is as big as 2 double-decker buses
It loves to eat people
It lives in a hole underground in Australia!

Amy Thompson
Codsall Middle School, Codsall

One Great Pounce!

His humongous tank as tall as can be!
Inside he was swimming, smiling too,
His lunch was fearfully frozen,
As silent as a tree he was so still.
All of a sudden he pounced on his lunch,
The fish was gone in one great munch!
I went to feed my great white narwhal,
He pulled my arm into his tank,
Then I was gone in one great munch!

Emilia Wiggin
Codsall Middle School, Codsall

Tioth

Tioth is a very peculiar pet
Maybe the most peculiar pet you've met!
He's small and loud
But us humans won't hear a sound...
He's marvellous and lazy
But maybe a little crazy?
He can bust some moves
In his tiny little shoes
I don't think Tioth will change to this day
But he's amazing in every way!

Chloe Elliman (10)
Codsall Middle School, Codsall

Rocky The Spy

R ichest pet alive in the world
O bey the lord, he does
C ute as a dog
K ing here
Y awning he does

T uxedo is what he wears
H ero spy
E xtraordinary he is

S neaking around
P retending to be a stuffed animal
Y ard is where he plays.

Jasper Lowe (9)
Codsall Middle School, Codsall

Unicorn Disco Rabbit

My unicorn rabbit Benji
He loves to disco and twirl
His favourite food is pig's bum
He loves trying different tutus on
He is a really lovely pet to have
He is very, very greedy
He loves going on his tiptoes
He wears a pink soft ballet dress
He loves every type of dancing
He has his wonderful sparkly disco ball!

Jessica Simmonds (10)
Codsall Middle School, Codsall

The Cagon

You walk into the sweet shop,
It just opened and you are as happy as can be,
But as soon as you walk in you can't believe your eyes!
For there, lollipop in paw, is a tiny green dragon!
Its whiskers twitch as it flutters over,
It hands you a sweet and waves goodbye,
For the tiny dragon vanishes,
Never to be seen again...

Willow Roalfe
Codsall Middle School, Codsall

Corndog

C orndog likes candyfloss
O nly in the summer months
R unning around at night, no time for sleep
N ever behaves herself, always gets told off
D ashing around the park, the fields and the garden
O r at the shopping centre in town
G etting some clothes, shoes or make-up!

Brooke Platt (10)
Codsall Middle School, Codsall

Panacat

P anacat likes pancakes
A nd it lives in a secret passageway to death
N o one can believe he is black, white, orange, yellow
A nd ginger!
C ome and see him now, you won't believe your eyes
A mazingly he likes to take a walk
T eaching him was so easy-peasy.

Jacob Holden (10)
Codsall Middle School, Codsall

Unlucky Duky

Unlucky Duky is the king of the lake
Wakes to a sun so so bright
He shoots some lasers from his eyes
People's bread is as soft as a pillow
But when he comes to have a bite
All hear screams left and right
But at 12am, dead of night
He spreads his wings and takes flight
Swoooosh!

Ben Robinson (9)
Codsall Middle School, Codsall

Super Lion Tiger

Super Lion Tiger is big and strong
They will always notice when people need help
They have super speed as fast as a bullet, probably even faster
They will do anything, even if it is something crazy!
They are my superhero pets
If you want they will be in the shops so come and get them quick!

Aarian Gill (9)
Codsall Middle School, Codsall

The Zebracorn

With a magical horn,
Here comes the zebracorn.
She's sassy like a model,
She is colourful like a rainbow in the sky.
She walks like a model,
But never wobbles.
She might be posh,
But when no one's there she acts like a monkey!
But she's cute and cuddly.

Lola Gillen (10)
Codsall Middle School, Codsall

Dogacorn

D ashing around the town
O n the lookout for a terrific thing
G oing home only when it's been found
A dventurous Dogacorn
C an't stay home
O nly when it rains
R eady to go out exploring
N ever on her own.

Danniella Shore (10)
Codsall Middle School, Codsall

Bella The Brilliant Bear

B ella the best of the best in fashion
E laborate, extraordinary and clever
L oving to sing, she can also be very mean
L ike a jelly bean, why can't she be clean?
A lso loving anything pretty, such as: jewellery, hats, shoes and so on!

Safa Qasim (9)
Codsall Middle School, Codsall

Bob The Misty Picklow

Bob the mystery picklow
Is my special pet
He lies around all day
Eating my cupcake buffet
Poos and wees he doesn't do
Instead he'd rather sneeze on my veggie stew
During the night he whines and wails
If he gets his cupcake stale!

Lola Jackson
Codsall Middle School, Codsall

Rad Sausage

R ad Sausage
A mazing pet
D o you want him?

S mells of sausages
A mazing beast
U nique animal
S mells nice
A ketchup launcher
G urgles loudly
E xcited animal!

Isaac Danbury (9)
Codsall Middle School, Codsall

Cookie

C ookie is a super cat that gives cats catnip cocktails that are
O ut of this world!
O kay, her hovering is so cool
K ids praise her
I nterviews are best for her
E specially her sidekick, the flying cocktail.

Rosie Sayers (9)
Codsall Middle School, Codsall

Turbo Tortoise

Whizz, off he goes, off on a run
And when he runs he's faster than a shot from a gun
And although he's shrivelled like a raisin
He's faster than a laser
And his shell is smooth like a bell
His house is inside his shell.

Reginald Myers (10)
Codsall Middle School, Codsall

Boris The Turtle

Boris the turtle was swimming in the ocean
He was as pale as sun lotion
His eyes shimmered in the sun like a plum
His head shrivelled like gum
His skin was green and when he got angry he talked mean
His shell was the colour of green beans.

Jacob Rhead (10)
Codsall Middle School, Codsall

Lazy Cat

L ying on the bed purring
A lways eating
Z oe is her name
Y oung she is, like a kitten

C omes to the cat bowl almost every minute
A lways thinking about fish
T hat's how she is!

Felix Davis (9)
Codsall Middle School, Codsall

Fredy The Transforming Pet

F earless puppy and not scared of anything
R ough, as if his skull is made out of concrete
E xtraordinary dog who fights evil
D evourer of the evil Mars warriors
Y oga expert to weaken enemies.

Sam Akers (9)
Codsall Middle School, Codsall

Tnake, The Naughtiest Animal In The Universe!

T errifying claws that scratch like daggers!
N aughty when he sees enemies!
A fraid, you might be!
K iller animal, beware!
E ating little children like a vicious, ferocious lion!

Avni Chodha (9)
Codsall Middle School, Codsall

Untitled

My zeb horse is different to others
He's incredible and funny, crazy and fast
He eats and sleeps all day long
He barks like mad all night until he's tired out
He walks by himself till morning rise.

JJ Garbett
Codsall Middle School, Codsall

Sparkle The Unicorn

Her curly hair is pearly in the sun
She has a pink apron and some ink
Her horn is very beautiful and suitable
She loves sausage and she lives in a cottage
Her eyes shine like stars, but she hates the park.

Ella-Mae Thompson-Wiggin (9)
Codsall Middle School, Codsall

Bilay

- **B** ilay
- **I** s a really good fish, he eats tropical fish food
- **L** ovely fish, he works as a sucker fish
- **A** baby fish
- **Y** oung fish, he is so fussy because he is on his own.

Reuben Price (9)
Codsall Middle School, Codsall

Wolfie The Mascot

W alks on the football pitch
O range and black stripes
L ines up to go
F abulous support to the team
I s the best
E xtraordinary mascot!

Austin Winwood (10)
Codsall Middle School, Codsall

Spicky

- **S** assy and dangerous
- **P** opular, as in famous
- **I** ncredibly wild and crazy
- **C** ool as a motor scooter
- **K** ind of a tomboy
- **Y** OLO, he screams!

Bronny Lloyd
Codsall Middle School, Codsall

Rocky The Great

R ocky the force field
O ff the charts of power
C uter than a dog
K ing of cats
Y ou'll never meet a better spy cat!

Liam Lewis (9)
Codsall Middle School, Codsall

Jermy

J oyful, admirable, clever fish
E xtraordinarily tiny fishy
R eally fast fish
M arvellous fish
Y ellow fish!

Charlie Deaville (9)
Codsall Middle School, Codsall

Tery

T errifically sassy
E motional
R idiculously weird
Y ou would be scared if you were with her when she is mad!

Amelia Hotchkiss (9)
Codsall Middle School, Codsall

Buster!

One day I got a dog
That looks like a log
He danced like a frog
He ran and ran like a mop
His fur was fuzzy like a tiger!

Harry Dornan (10)
Codsall Middle School, Codsall

Fad

F ad is fat and grumpy
A n angry, wild animal
D aft, gigantic, enormous Fad!

Arjan Bassi (9)
Codsall Middle School, Codsall

Oreo The Goaton

O reo is a goaton, which is a goat and a dragon
R eally fast he goes to the theme park
E ating fish and seeds is his favourite thing to do
O reo is big so he has a shrink ray

T he best thing about him is his flying
H e has red scales and feathered wings
E veryone thinks he is cute!

G row button he uses when he is small
O nly one I love the most
A dorable wings that sparkle in the sun
T he jokes he tells make me laugh
O reo has a lot of fluffy friends
N o one can beat my Oreo!

Jack Poxon (11)
Elmwood School, Walsall

Terror Tortoise

T error is his name
E ggs are his favourite food
R eactor to fights
R earranging his books
O range hands
R eally sharp teeth

T rustful of the night
O verall great
R eally has no mates
T imid and furry
O range and scary
I nstead of being a fairy
S lick he looks
E ats like us.

Carson Price (12)
Elmwood School, Walsall

Freddy The Cat

Freddy is my friend
Freddy is really naughty in the night
Freddy is really good in the day
Freddy dances at night
Freddy dances any time he wants
Freddy is a lovely cat

Freddy likes to eat a lot of stuff
Freddy likes being hot
Freddy likes lights

Freddy is a good cat
Freddy can sometimes be naughty
Freddy is a good and naughty cat at the same time!

Cody Love-Knight
Elmwood School, Walsall

Snarrot

S eeds and bacon are what he likes to eat
N eeding rest, four hours a day, so don't make a peep
A lways playing the most fun games
R ichard is history which he uses as a decoy
R unning from the bath and very hard to catch
O nly angry people wouldn't want a snarrot
T omorrow I think I will get another.

Francis Gosling
Elmwood School, Walsall

Muffins

M y pet Muffins eats cake
U nder the stars is where we bake
F luffy fur makes me feel calm
F luffy claws cause me no harm
I want to take Muffins to the park
N ot in the day only in the dark
S o no one can see us bake under the stars.

Logan Hawley (11)
Elmwood School, Walsall

The Snaion

S and makes the Snaion happy
N its always get in his fur
A t night he goes to hunt deer
I t loves to jump-scare people
O nions make it angry
N ot to be messed with unless you want to lose your head!

Tyler-Reece Jones (11)
Elmwood School, Walsall

Snek

S uper long like spaghetti
N ight-time is the right time for Snek
E ggs are his favourite snack
K ing Snek is nocturnal like a cat.

Sennen Gregory (11)
Elmwood School, Walsall

Lisy The Levitating Lizard!

L isy is my pet
I love her with all my heart
S he and me go to the shops
Y es, oh yes we have fun!

Dilan Smith (11)
Elmwood School, Walsall

Unifluffles The Superhero!

U nder the roof of her house, Unifluffles watched the rain pour onto her window
N ever did she think she would stay in for this long! Two weeks!
I nside her house she had done a lot of things, but she couldn't think of anything to do now
F orever she had wished to be a superhero, but now she wasn't getting the chance to!
L ittle poor Unifluffles was so sad. But one day...
U nifluffles couldn't stand this anymore, so she used her powers to stop the rain!
F luffles (that's her nickname) actually did it, she didn't think she would!
F inally she could become a superhero!
L uckily there was a supervillain in town. A few minutes later she had defeated the supervillain!
E ven though she didn't have many superpowers, she was very popular now
S o whenever there was a supervillain in town she would defeat them and everyone in town lived happily ever after!

Seren Pantall (10)
Halfway Primary School, Llanelli

Crazy Coco

C razy Coco flies over the field of cupcakes
R unning over the rooftops where there's gingerbread gumdrops
A gingerbread man coming from the gummy graveyard
Z ombies coming from the gummy graveyard
Y o-Yo Bears coming from the Snickers Swamp

C razy Coco flying to Mars Meadows
O h phew, she's finally safe
C razy Coco has now fallen asleep
O h no, she is now snoring!

Annabelle O'Neill (9)
Halfway Primary School, Llanelli

Potion The Cool Dog!

P otion is evil, you have got to know that!
O n Planet Shards, I'm his evil owner!
T o be his friend you have to know him well!
I n the evening he prowls through the mist!
O n Planet Shards, he's the guardian!
N ow you have got to know, evil is his character flaw!

Maia Jones (9)
Halfway Primary School, Llanelli

Fireball

F ierce sarcasm when you say something stupid
I n the dark
R ebels fear the grasp of Fireball
E verybody loves her (except for the criminals!)
B ella the cat is her sidekick
A ll the world worships her
L ovely
L ittle hero that is her.

Fern Prescott (9)
Halfway Primary School, Llanelli

All About My Kittycorn

K ittycorns are cute
I f they get some attitude
T ell them what to do
T ell them, don't get angry
Y ou can give advice
C an I have some food, please?
O f course you can
R ight, are you okay
N ow?

Olivia Lewis
Halfway Primary School, Llanelli

Polly Parrot

P olly is so cute and fun to play with
O nly thing is she hates my zebra finches
L icking scrambled egg is her favourite
L ying down and scratching her belly is what she loves
Y ellow, black and brown are her colours.

Harri Howells
Halfway Primary School, Llanelli

Bella

B ella is playful, Bella is fun, Bella is cute, Bella is messy
E lla is her friend, they play all the time
L ucy's her sister
L ucas is her brother
A nd they lived happily ever after.

Megan Lemon (9)
Halfway Primary School, Llanelli

Rocco Rockstar's Fashion Show

He's become Harry Potter
He has a scar
And he plays the guitar
The stage is full
Lots of costumes
Who's he going to pick?
It's the annoying dino bro!
The crowd scream, "Wow!"

Ollie Grant (9)
Halfway Primary School, Llanelli

Jeff The Dog

J eff is playful and wild
E very day Jeff comes to me and jumps on me
F ish is his favourite food to eat
F ood goes all over the floor and me!

Rocco Thomas (10)
Halfway Primary School, Llanelli

Rosey

Rosey is so cute
And so happy and fluffy
She's so so cute
And an eater and fast runner!
Even my bestie
But just lazy
Rosey is a cute girl to me.

Riley Hanley (10)
Halfway Primary School, Llanelli

Rock 'n' Roll

Hello everyone, I am Rex the rockstar,
You will love me, I am the best pop star.
I am a clever and cool dog,
With fur as brown as a log.
My golden glasses are shaped like a star,
And they are as shiny as a brand new car.
I hope you like my black glittery jacket,
And don't forget to check out my silver locket.
Sometimes I like to sing when it's sunny,
And sometimes I can be really funny.
You will be amazed to watch me dance and sing,
When my favourite guitar goes *ding, ding, ding!*
The population of my noisy fans is very large,
Because I'm the one in charge.
I love rocking on the colossal stage,
And I never want to go back to that stinky cage.

Priyanka Kala (8)
Krishna Avanti Primary School, Evington

Severious The Savvy Snake

I am an intriguing sly snake,
I can make you fear and shake.
With scaly skin smooth like a winter sweater,
Having a tummy full makes me feel better.
I am a reptile, in humid regions found,
When people see me, they go around.
As green as evergreen leaves, I live in arched trees,
In grass, sand and seas.

I have skin covered with scales:
Which is either patterned or pale.
With radiant colours and a lovely shine,
Around the tree branches I often entwine.

I coil and slither;
My prey I bite and smother.
Swishing and slashing through the branches I squeeze,
I spy on my target with tremendous expertise.
My deadly fangs don't miss,
Take it as a warning when I hiss.

With a lengthy forked tongue, I smell,
I have no legs or ears as well.
I gobble my food whole,
Whether that's a human or a mole.

It's amazing to see me shed my skin,
Anaconda and venomous cobras are my kin.
In your garden, if you find me,
Please kindly don't mind me.
Simply stand still on the grass,
And allow me to briskly pass.

Payal Keshvala (8)
Krishna Avanti Primary School, Evington

My Incredible Pet Flies!

Guinea pig! Unicorn! Caterpillar!
Flying over the moon, flying over the moon,
Harmony Harper, the Catunipig, flies over the moon.
With its ginormous wings and enchanted unicorn horn,
it flies over the moon.
With its guinea pig face and caterpillar body,
it squeaks, squeaks, squeaks!

My cute, adorable pet gives me a ride up in the sky!
This one and only clever pet flies around loop-the-loop,
over the rainbows and over the moon!
An extraordinary animal, people see zooming around the apple tree.
Who is the owner of this incredible pet?
Not you, not she, not he,
Me!

My pet named Harmony Harper is excellent at cuddling.
You can fly on this humongous pet to the moon and back.
My extraordinary Catunipig is simply remarkable and super special to me.

Anaya Kishori Dasi (9)
Krishna Avanti Primary School, Evington

Rock Star Casper The Dog

His name is Casper,
He thinks he's dapper,
But not a good rapper.

He loves to play the guitar,
That's why he became a rock star,
He only sings about food,
When he's in a good mood,
Or else he can be rude.

When he has a dare,
He thinks about his blue hair.

Seeing as he's really tiny,
He's also really shiny,

His sunglasses are still shining,
Especially when he's in the lighting.

He's sassy, mostly to his masses,
He's adorable but not so affordable.

He's so furry but
He's always in a hurry,

He's always messy,
Especially when he is with his friend Tessy.

Leah Mapara (8)
Krishna Avanti Primary School, Evington

My White Unicorn

My unicorn hops, skips, jumps and bounces,
My pet twitches its nose and pounces.

Her eyes are deep brown like a tree log,
Her fur is white, soft and misty like fog.

She loves fruit and vegetables but her favourite is carrots,
I love her more than anything, even more than parrots.

My unicorn's tail makes a variety of Pringles,
And when I eat it, my mouth tingles.

She has a golden, bright, sparkly horn,
But it is pointy and sharper than a thorn.

She is cuddly and snuggly,
And really sweet and lovely.

Her mane is baby pink,
And her hair glows to make me a bubbly drink.

Elissia Dharamshi (8)
Krishna Avanti Primary School, Evington

The Phenomenal Penguin

My pet is extraordinary,
She has some specialities
I love my penguin
But she does some cheeky sins
Her name is Lisa,
She would love to meet ya
She loves going out on a sunny day
And all she does is play!
Her belly is a clock
When people see her they get a shock!
She has duck feet that help her swim
And they get very strong in the gym
Lisa has scaly snake arms
But she doesn't have any palms
She has amazing antennae which give her Wi-Fi
She's very sci-fi!
The most amazing feature of all is her mind-controlling goggles!
It's like she's a superhero in a novel!
I love my pet!

Riaa Kotecha (11)
Krishna Avanti Primary School, Evington

My Bad Pet!

My pet is a very bad pet,
He is so scary he gives me a threat.
He has big, orange, fierce eyes,
You may not believe me but you'll be surprised.
My pet's body is very rough,
You haven't seen it but he is tough.
He has sharp and pointy claws,
He also has teeth in his smelly jaws.
Yesterday, me and my pet did a dance,
We never knew we did it in France.
We met my friend just down the street,
And we sat down in the hot boiling heat.
My friend was shocked about the pet I had,
But she never knew it was very bad.
My pet is a big monster,
I wish he was eaten by a big lobster!

Esha Modha (8)
Krishna Avanti Primary School, Evington

The Day I Met Fantastiko!

I was strolling through the park when I saw something strange.
It had the face of a panda, but when I blinked it changed!

Suddenly it grew angel wings, they were colossal in size.
Then it let out an enormous yawn and its teeth looked like French fries!

Its body had the shape of a bright blue bear.
It looked so peculiar and furry, it was hard not to stare.

When it walked it waddled like a duck.
If you touched its webbed feet it would bring you luck.

There was a spike on its head that looked like an ice cream cone.
We became best of friends and it followed me home!

Khushi Parekh
Krishna Avanti Primary School, Evington

Cake Cackler

C ake Cackler's teeny tiny
A nd can be extremely slimy
K eeping content and remaining adventurous
E ven his methods are rather ungenerous

C reating a scene is really marvellous
A nd deceiving others can become larcenous
C reating appearances of being very gentle
K eeping in truth he is severely mental
L ike himself his instincts are crazy
E ver like his lifestyle, he is extremely lazy
R emembering his plots but his memories are hazy.

So here is Cake Cackler,
His favourite flower is a daisy.

Alisha Mistry (10)
Krishna Avanti Primary School, Evington

My Dancing Pug, Coco

Coco the pug likes to hug, she loves to dance; it's like she's in a trance.

When she's in the mood, she will groove, groove, groove and when you play her favourite song, she will merrily sing along.

She loves to samba and dances to a fabulous mamba!

Coco has a tutu and a little fancy crown and if you do not clap to her dance, she gives a sad, sad frown.

Coco is a clever girl; she is sassy and wild,
We always have a disco that is classy and styled.

I love my pet pug Coco, she is totally unique,
I would hate to have a slimy and spotty three-eyed freak!

Riya Mandalia (8)
Krishna Avanti Primary School, Evington

Funny Little Fiona

F lying is quite good, although I don't know how she can fly
U nique is something she's good at or maybe she's just different
N oisy she is all around the house and also outside too
N osy, she is nosy, she likes to spy on people
Y oung because she's only a kid

F unny indeed, she is funny
I maginative Fiona imagines everything can happen
O utstanding she is when she does somersaults
N oble but she can also be a bit silly
A ppreciative, very, very appreciative or maybe not.

Diya B Modhwadia (8)
Krishna Avanti Primary School, Evington

Magical Fish

Once I got a fish which was magical,
He could swim really fast with his bright golden fins,
He also had magical blue eyes which would shine through the sea,
I love my fish the most in the world.

I wish it would fly in the sky.
I wish to go to school with him.
I wish him to climb up the mountain.
I love my fish the most in the world.

There are oceans, there are seas,
There are rivers, there are lakes,
There are ponds, there are streams,
But the best I like is the fishbowl in my home.
I love my fish the most in the world.

Vivaan Jhala (7)
Krishna Avanti Primary School, Evington

Super Lavender

S uper Lavender is super strong
U p and down she flies all day long
P owers she uses to save the day
E ven if she does not get paid
R eally marvellous and incredible, as she is a super cat!

L avender likes to love and care
A nd she always likes to share
V ery kind she is indeed
E ven if she reveals her true identity
N ow she has grown
D esperately she never moans
E very day, she helps indeed
R eally furry and really clever, as she is Super Lavender!

Aarya Patel (9)
Krishna Avanti Primary School, Evington

My Dog Is My Friend

My dog is the most precious animal of all,
He doesn't just follow and grab a ball,
With eyes open wide,
He hunts when I hide,
He achieves spectacular tricks,
Builds me camps out of sticks,
He'd never rumble, scratch or even bite,
But frighten my friends if they fight,
His nose is short and scrubby,
His ears hang rather low,
And he always brings the stick back,
No matter how far you throw,
My dog is my very best friend,
And I will look after him until the end.

Pavitra Patel (9)
Krishna Avanti Primary School, Evington

The Rockstar Hedgehog

As Hedgehog drove in his Mustang car,
He was proud of becoming a rockstar,
His wife, Panda, was at home,
Whilst his favourite footballer was on loan,
He had two wonderful kids,
That liked to play with steel lids,

Hedgehog had ten tentacles on his hips,
Because he loved eating chilli chips,
He was covered in black and white stripes,
He also had plenty of purple spikes,
This rockstar had horns on top of his eyes,
His cousin, Koala, loved chomping on Pukka pies.

Dilan Chauhan (9)
Krishna Avanti Primary School, Evington

Figgy The Feline

Oh Figgy, oh Figgy, as cute as he can be,
Fantastic Figgy loves to catch mice and put them between his teeth,
Figgy's favourite food is prawns,
Whenever he sees any in his dish,
He gobbles them down very quick!
Figgy is very protective of his territory for as long as he can,
As soon as he sees a fox,
He sprints back inside, shying away into his box,
Figgy the hyperactive cat,
Just purely loves to play,
Until he's exhausted which is always by the end of the day.

Mitali Patel (8)
Krishna Avanti Primary School, Evington

Wolferbutterfly

W ild, weird Wolfer
O n the treetop
L azing around
F urry and feathery
E xtraordinarily cute
R ising high in the sky
B asking in the sun
U nder the sunny sky
T asting the juicy nectar
T umbling down the treetop
E ating away insects
R adiant, shiny, furry
F lying up and down
L ying by my side
Y et I love him so much.

Siya Anadkat (7)
Krishna Avanti Primary School, Evington

My Frightening Pet!

My pet, don't even ask why
He'll boil you like a fry
Oh really you wanna try
Then get down and cry.

He'll punch you like a hammer
He'll scam all your devices like a scammer
He'll slam you to the ground like a slammer
So hard that you'll forget all your grammar!

My pet, he's a lion
He's as strong as iron
The colour of his eyes are cyan
And he speaks Hawaiian!

Ansh Shah (9)
Krishna Avanti Primary School, Evington

Puppy Disco

Purry the puppy was bored, so then she saw a bee,
The bee took Purry to a place and she saw a key,
The key was glowing with colours,
Purry touched the key and ended up in a disco,
Purry was in disco clothes, she said, "Let's go."
Purry had lots of fun,
And the lights were beautiful, shimmering lights,
And they were bright,
By the time it had been an hour,
It took them back and Purry wanted a shower.

Khunti (8)
Krishna Avanti Primary School, Evington

Where Are You My Rabbit?

As soon as I looked under the bed
Which was bloody red
I checked under the table
Nearly fell 'cause of the annoying cable

I started to get scared
I felt that before I did not care
I really, really missed her
All of a sudden, I found a trail of her fur

I felt a massive smile on my face
As I tied up my lace
Before my eyes I saw my rabbit
Who was sat on my jacket
I love my pet!

Bhavani Nayee (10)
Krishna Avanti Primary School, Evington

Marley & Mimi

Marley eats, sleeps
And loves his treats.
Marley loves cuddles
And is attracted to puddles.
Marley loves to climb trees
But always leaves his peas.
Marley was born on a farm
And his nature is very calm.
Mimi is cute but mute,
Mimi is white and brown
And acts like a clown.
Mimi has little paws,
And likes to play outdoors
Marley and Mimi are my pets,
I think they are the best.

Anya Sawjani (9)
Krishna Avanti Primary School, Evington

Hashtag Husky

HH is snow-white
She travels on planes and helicopters
Believes herself to be utterly bright
But truly her personality is appalling

Amongst the fur are hidden spikes
Used to hurt everyone and anyone
Which gets her lots of TikTok likes
But of the very wrong type

She squeaks like a mouse
When she is afraid
So she lives with her twin in an adorable house
In the middle of Pup City!

Divya Chauhan (10)
Krishna Avanti Primary School, Evington

Sparky The Parrot

Sparky the parrot loves to eat lots of carrots,
She is colourful and bright,
But she hates shiny light during the night,
Sparky likes to play peekaboo,
When she sees you anew,
Sparky is an intelligent bird,
From far away she can be heard.
Sparky's wings are long and wide,
She likes to flutter them all the time on the side.
Sparky's feathers glisten in the morning sun like a cup of hot tea.

Nihal Jitesh Patel (8)
Krishna Avanti Primary School, Evington

Furry, My Friend

I have a friend who's soft and small
I have a friend who comes when I call
I have a friend who lives in a tree
I have a friend whose brother's name is Lee
I have a friend who can see in the dark
I have a friend who loves to eat bark
I have a friend who jumps really high
I have a friend who wears a tie
I have a friend who loves curry
I have a friend whose name is Furry!

Dhruvi Sani (7)
Krishna Avanti Primary School, Evington

The Rescue Rabbit

J umpy
E nergetic
N aughty
N onchalant
Y oung

Jenny, Jenny,
She weighs a penny,
She jumps higher and higher,
Until she sees fire,
But Jenny knows what to do,
She hops and hops,
Until she stops,
And people shout,
"Jenny, Jenny, come rescue me!"
The rescue rabbit saves the day,
So come and make way.

Shania Desai (8)
Krishna Avanti Primary School, Evington

Buttercup, My Adorable Little Puppy!

Buttercup is colourful and stripy
But sometimes she can be cheeky
She likes cuddles and likes jumping in puddles!

Her talent is sport
And when she plays tag she likes being caught
Buttercup is really adorable
And that makes her memorable!

She is really gentle
With a stinging nettle
Her fur is softer than a koala
But she is frightened of lava!

Dhriti Lakhani (10)
Krishna Avanti Primary School, Evington

Catzila The Villain

Beware of Catzila's toxic wings,
Otherwise, you'll be saying hello to the worst trillion kings.

Don't look into its flaming eyes,
Or you'll be saying the bye-byes.

Look out for its venomous fangs,
Otherwise, you'll be gone in twenty bangs.

Don't get touched by its spiky tail,
Or else you'll never get your important mail.

Rahul Nathwani (9)
Krishna Avanti Primary School, Evington

Super Puppy

W ardoole is a dog in daylight
A nd a super puppy at night
R ides an aeroplane and saves the day
D oes stunts in different ways
O ver the moon, it goes shining like a star
O h, it's so adorable, it will melt your heart
L ives like there is no tomorrow
E very day is a new adventure because my dog is a superhero!

Isha Soni (10)
Krishna Avanti Primary School, Evington

Tigi - My Mysterious Pet

Tigi is a spotty and stripy animal
You can ride on his back like a camel
You can also climb on his neck
Just like a ladder

Tigi is cleverer than a monkey
And is stronger than a donkey
Tigi is furrier than a bear
And loves eating pears

Tigi is an omnivore
Which makes him strong
Tigi can stand on two legs
With an egg on his head.

Nevaan Lakhani (7)
Krishna Avanti Primary School, Evington

My Clever Koala

I'm a koala whose name is Cutie Pie,
I'm very smart so I wear a tie.

I like to play football,
Because I never fall.

I can shoot lava,
When I eat a guava.

I'm very funny,
When I jump like a bunny.

I'm a wizard,
So I can make a blizzard.

Hey buddy, make me your pet,
And your life will be set.

Aaryan Bapodra (9)
Krishna Avanti Primary School, Evington

Dancing Unicorn

The magic is inside you,
You can do whatever you want to do.
Put on your crown,
And turn around.
You're a queen,
It's not a dream.
You're marvellous, adorable, incredible too,
So go and put on your sparkly shoe.
Stand up high,
And reach the sky.
Soon you'll feel above the clouds,
Well done! We're so proud.

Shruti Karelia (8)
Krishna Avanti Primary School, Evington

My Pet Rhino

I once had an extraordinary rhino
His name was Mino
He went to school
With someone cool
He worked at the zoo
Where the monkeys said, "Boo!"
He went to space
In a race
He flew in a gigantic rocket
His shorts had a soft pocket
He landed on Mars
There were no cars
He went back home
With an adorable gnome!

Niya Patel (8)
Krishna Avanti Primary School, Evington

The Clumsy Hippo

Thump, thump, thump,
Bump, bump, bump,
All jump, jump, jump,
Ouch, ouch, ouch,
Hippo's coming on her way,
She'll stomp us down to the ground.

But in the night,
When the moon is bright,
And the stars are light,
Hippo becomes light,
She'll put her dancing shoes on,
And dance away while the night goes on.

Jhanvi Vyas (8)
Krishna Avanti Primary School, Evington

Kittycorn

Kittycorn, Kittycorn, where are you at?
Where are you going and why?
How does your horn sparkle like that?
Your wings are so colourful as you pass by.
Why are you waving your tail in the air?
Why are your eyes wide open in a stare?
You purr,
You play,
You sleep,
You leap.

(A Kittycorn is a cat and a unicorn combined.)

Pia Mistry (10)
Krishna Avanti Primary School, Evington

Peggy The Penguin

My odd little pet is very lovely,
She is warm and extremely cuddly.

Her name is Peggy and she is a penguin, don't you know?
I've had her since she was a baby and watched her grow.

Peggy loves the warm,
But all the other penguins like a storm.

Penguins like to huddle up tight,
But Peggy likes to have a fight!

Anya Kotecha (7)
Krishna Avanti Primary School, Evington

Glowbert

Glowbert the turtle lives on a beach,
And he comes out at night to eat a great big peach.
When he is funny, he gets bright and sunny,
When he is too cute, people give him fruit.
Because he is adorable, he is so portable,
He is incredible and he is inedible.
Overall, Glowbert loves to chill,
As he glows in the dark with his shell.

Yogiraj Dixit (9)
Krishna Avanti Primary School, Evington

Star, My Special Cat

This is a poem about my cat
She always sleeps on a mat

My cat is furry and so sweet
Whilst she is purry she needs a big seat

My cat is cute and wears a pretty suit
That's tiny and shiny

My cat, Star
Knows how to drive a fast car

This is a poem about my cat
She always sleeps on a mat.

Harini Vinothkumar (9)
Krishna Avanti Primary School, Evington

My Best Stylish Pet

B eautiful beaunicorn
E ndless legs
A mazing long hair
U nbelievably she can fly to the sky
N ight-time she plays
I love to ride her
C ome and see my peculiar pet
O n her horn magic dust appears
R iding her is so much fun
N ext to her, I feel very safe.

Keshavi Naker (8)
Krishna Avanti Primary School, Evington

Amir Has Gone Missing!

My dog was fierce
But he left me in tears
He was a house guard
And he worked so hard

He loves to eat bones
And he never moans
My dog never bites
And he loves to chase kites

I love my dog
He always brings me a log
I hope he comes home
Because he's a dog he doesn't have a phone.

Devraj Nayee (8)
Krishna Avanti Primary School, Evington

Acrobat Fluffy

A dorable
C harming
R uns like a cheetah
O utstanding as the sun
B eautiful as a rainbow
A crobatic as a monkey
T ough as a lion

F un
L oving
U nbelievable
F unky
F unny
Y outhful, acrobatic Fluffy!

Ayanna Kotecha (7)
Krishna Avanti Primary School, Evington

Rocksy The Rock Star!

R espectful and kind, she will always be divine
O ptimistic about the day, always wanting to play
C lever and cute, happy all the time
K araoke she loves, her favourite birds are doves
S assy and popular, just like me
Y outhful and truthful, she will always be very playful.

Disha Ranpura (9)
Krishna Avanti Primary School, Evington

My Incredible Pet

I have a pet named Roxy,
She loved drinking cola and Pepsi,
Her favourite colour was red,
And her favourite place was bed,
She was cute as a baby,
But was as fierce as a lion maybe,
She would be reading a story,
But only if they had a glory,
Have you ever heard of a pet like this, maybe?

Neeva Shah (8)
Krishna Avanti Primary School, Evington

Mischievous Muffin

My pet's name is Muffin
He is always rockin'.

He is my superhero
He always listens to our stereo.

His favourite food is roasted dingo
And he likes to bingo.

But when he drives
He can crash into beehives.

He is the best
As he is always in my nest!

Nandakishore Mundalappa (8)
Krishna Avanti Primary School, Evington

Tarantula

T errifying as a tiger
A dventurous as an explorer
R uthless like a streetfighter
A gile as a mountain climber
N octurnal as a wolf
T ough as a gorilla
U npredictable like the weather
L ively like a firework
A stonishing like a star.

Shriya Solanki (8)
Krishna Avanti Primary School, Evington

Cat In Many Hats

Lloyd is our cat
Who likes wearing hats

He has a ninja mask
And uses it for his task

His eyes are green
And have a beam

He likes the night
As much as he likes the fight

He also likes to wander around the house
And he is scared of the big, hairy mouse.

Shivam Mistry (8)
Krishna Avanti Primary School, Evington

Gizmo

Bark! That's what they love!
They get out of bed, bed, bed
Lazy Gizmo went for a walk, walk, walk
He played, played, played
He chased everyone like a cheetah
Gizmo ate until his stomach popped!
The dancing dog ran, ran, ran like a mouse
To his extraordinary gigantic house!

Aditya Madhwani (7)
Krishna Avanti Primary School, Evington

Randy

My pet is called Randy,
He loves cotton candy,
He is a panda cub,
And sleeping he loves,
He is cute and smart,
And he's not afraid of the dark,
Randy is clever and not bad at art,
And he always plays with a plastic cart,
My pet is called Randy,
And he loves cotton candy.

Hashini Vinoth Kumar (9)
Krishna Avanti Primary School, Evington

Fred The Frog

I saw a frog
Who was sitting on a log!

His name was Fred
And was lying in a dirty shed.

He looked so soggy
And was looking at a doggy.

He was extremely sad
As all the animals thought he was mad.

I saw a frog
Who was sitting on a log!

Kush Popat (8)
Krishna Avanti Primary School, Evington

Rocky The Lion

I love to hear your ferocious roar all day long,
When you roar, everyone runs away as fast as a cheetah,
You are the king who wears no crown,
Rocky, you are the best pet around,
Rocky, you are a big and strong lion,
With a magnificent mane of golden-brown hair.

Anay Mistry (9)
Krishna Avanti Primary School, Evington

A Weird Pet

Listening to this poem, you may think pets are weird,
But don't fill yourself with worry, they cannot be feared,
This pet is one of a kind,
He has a long, twisted tail which is amazing and could make you blind,
Amazing and kind,
You'll be colour-blind.

Neha Bharakhada (8)
Krishna Avanti Primary School, Evington

My Enchanti!

E nchanted and magical
N ice and mean
C ourageous and strong
H appy and angry
A mazing and boring
N aughty and behaving
T all and short
I ncredible and amazing

And this is Enchanti!

Kalindi Priya Carrillo (9)
Krishna Avanti Primary School, Evington

Helephant

H uge and hovering
E ye in the sky
L et it fly high
E xtraordinary and marvellous
P erfect and peculiar
H elping the police
A dorable and incredible
N ever fearful
T ell me its name.

Avi Patel (8)
Krishna Avanti Primary School, Evington

Ac-Rabbit

A nd a hop over here
C atch and a flip

R abbits over here and they are over there
A nd start all again
B ounce about
B ounce, bounce
I love to hop and bounce and wiggle around my
T ail.

Shanaya Kotecha (10)
Krishna Avanti Primary School, Evington

I Love My Pet!

P ets are helpful
E ven if you don't think so
T hey take care and cuddle you when you are lonely

L ove your pet
O ur pets deserve care
V ets take care of pets
E verybody take care of pets.

Keya Joshi (8)
Krishna Avanti Primary School, Evington

Goldie The Gold Rabbit

G oldie is the best pet
O nly her eyes are red
L ook, they glow in the dark
D ollies, that's what she plays with
I t's so cool because she can fly
E at your food Goldie, she's such a fussy rabbit.

Cherry-Mae Kotecha (8)
Krishna Avanti Primary School, Evington

Sausigo

- **S** mart and sassy Sausigo
- **A** mazing and adorable
- **U** ltimate, unique Sausigo
- **S** mall, slim Sausigo
- **I** ncredibly charming Sausigo
- **G** entle but clever Sausigo
- **O** bedient and obliging Sausigo.

Tanish Patel (8)
Krishna Avanti Primary School, Evington

The Great Eagleair

The best pet called Eagleair,
He is so strong and so fair,
He flies so fast,
Even faster than Dash,
He is so dangerous,
Sometimes he gets so furious,
He is very wild,
Sometimes he behaves like a child.

Heerav Chudasama (8)
Krishna Avanti Primary School, Evington

Brandy

B e brave pets
R egular pets will do
A nd you will be successful pets
N ot fancy, just any
D o you treat your pets kindly?
Y ou know they have feelings.

Mahi Parmar (8)
Krishna Avanti Primary School, Evington

My Friend Birep

B e aware
I t's a ferocious creature
R are in this country
E ndless flyer
P arrot kind

Look around you... there's one under your bed!

Janvi Khunti (10)
Krishna Avanti Primary School, Evington

Fuzzy Pants The DJ Rabbit

F urry
U nique
Z appy
Z esty
Y outhful

P eculiar
A mbitious
N atural
T alented
S tylish!

Anaya Ramaiya (7)
Krishna Avanti Primary School, Evington

My Beautiful Dog

My little dog is cute and sweet,
It is not very easy to even beat.
My little dog likes to play,
Every single day.
My little puppy likes to sleep,
He has a deep sleep.

Dilan Rana (9)
Krishna Avanti Primary School, Evington

Hero Bongo

B ig, strong, tough and huge
O range, brown, fuzzy and puffy
N ever down, strong and right
G iant, tall and big
O n to sing, ready to party.

Heer Jethwa (8)
Krishna Avanti Primary School, Evington

The Dog

This dog is fluffy
Like a puppy
The dog howls
Like a howling owl
This dog is stripy
Like a tiger
This dog is cute
Like a cute bunny.

Riya Mistry
Krishna Avanti Primary School, Evington

Dan The Dalmatian

Late, late, late,
Dan was late,
He was supposed to make a film for section B8.
He got his keys and got in his car,
Whoosh! He was off like a shooting star!
Dan was slim and very thick,
He needed to get to the studio quick!
He parked up and stopped the gear,
Where was Dan? everyone feared.
Dan set his camera at the speed of light,
Soon enough the film took flight.
He got his computer and tapped 'send'
Did the people like it? Was it the end?
They had a celebration,
And that's the story of the silly Dalmatian,
That was late, late, late!

Enzo Lanzetta (10)
Partney CE (A) Primary School, Partney

The Pink Bearded Pig

My bearded pig is pink and can fly
He watches sad films, eats Wotsits and cries
He went outside and flew with the wind
Whoosh, whoosh, whoosh!
While he did all sorts of silly things
My bearded pig grew bigger and bigger
He also grew slicker
But every night when I was asleep
Into the cupboard he would peek
My bearded pig has stubby toes
When he flew they cracked off
Crack, crack, crack
One night he flew in the dark
Hit a tree and all he could see was dark
Thud, thud, thud
The next morning he woke up in bed
Then he realised he was in a surgeon's care
He gulped, gulped, gulped
Screamed and shouted for help

That night he felt all good and neat
Came home and watched a video on how to be
Great, great, great!

Oscar Morris (10)
Partney CE (A) Primary School, Partney

Tizzy Wizzy The Magical Black Labrador

In the day Tizzy is a normal black Labrador
But at night the fun begins
First he attaches his cape
Then he gets his magical bone
And then the woof wand
Which doesn't start the fun yet
With a scratch of his bottom
Then the magic begins!
In the night he fights evil cat dragons
And saves dogs in distress
To get what all dog wizards want
Their magic hat
But one night I went to get a drink when he was putting on his cape
And guess what?
When he saw me he grinned
And he let me go with him
And guess what?

I helped him get his wizard hat
And I got one too
Now we fight cat dragons together
In the night!

Fraiser Lyall (10)
Partney CE (A) Primary School, Partney

Storm The Stormy Koala

My koala is slow.
He is grumpy.
He huffs, he puffs.
He sighs, he whines.
He likes to grumble.
And he likes to groan.
But oh, does he have a secret?
When no one is looking he raises his paws and...
One, two, three!
Rain, sleet, snow.
Sunshine and clouds.
Thunder and lightning.
He can do it all!
Little sparkles of pride dance in his eyes
As he watches the weather thrive!
My koala is slow and grumpy.
He huffs, he puffs.
He sighs and whines.
But he has a secret, a secret you can't tell...
Shhh!

Lois Louth (9)
Partney CE (A) Primary School, Partney

Fizz The Sloth

His miniature fluffy nose is surrounded by a bright faint face,
Massive beady eyes to scan for safety,
He has a velvety pink stomach in the middle of his beautiful body,
Perfect pale paws connect comfortably to his short arms,
Sleek, wavy legs underneath the skinny stomach,
He is the best companion you could have,
In the dark he is your light, he is brighter than a bedside lamp,
He is as cute as a baby,
That is my peculiar pink sloth.

Abigail Sands (11)
Partney CE (A) Primary School, Partney

Little Timmy

A goofy, always tired little fish
With an eye for everything
My little fish is the best
But he did get a bit angry when his new tank didn't arrive
Oh boy, trust me, you wouldn't have wanted to be there!
He's always tired
But if he's awake (which is very uncommon)
And you walk past
You'll be there for the next 2-3 hours chatting
As he swims around
You can see his sleek, shiny scales shimmer.
Bye!

Peter Gates (10)
Partney CE (A) Primary School, Partney

Dogon The Dragon

The dark, daring, dangerous dragon is gentle,
But when he hunts he's a ferocious wolf,
He's got razor-sharp claws that can slice you in half,
And puncture your lungs.
When he is under attack, he aggressively flies away.
The fluffy long tail will tie you up like a snake,
The tail will whip you and cut your arm off.
When he stomps, his fat, bulky legs make an earthquake,
His red beady eyes are like lasers.

Ethan Turner (10)
Partney CE (A) Primary School, Partney

King Bunny

I've got a king bunny
He has a boring, bulky body on his massive furry feet
He side bounces furiously
As his soft bossy cape swishes and swirls
As he bounces on the trampoline
Ready to do a front top tip
He bounces gracefully back to his room
Ready for me to give him nice furry cuddles
His spiky bright golden crown pricks me
I have to take it off
And his ears just flop!

Phoebe Lennon (10)
Partney CE (A) Primary School, Partney

Majestic Miranda

My peculiar pet is so small,
A fluffy rainbow tail,
And a long sleek rainbow body,
Pearl-white wings with a dot of silver,
Majestic blue eyes as blue as the sea,
She's called Miranda,
She quickly walks,
Very hyper,
And when it comes to walks - *whoosh!*
She slowly flies into the depths of the deep blue sky,
My peculiar pet is perfect just the way she is.

Lilli Edwards (10)
Partney CE (A) Primary School, Partney

Dog Who

I have a pet, an imaginative pet
He loves to watch TV and act out the scenes
In lockdown he watched this series called Doctor Who
And now he's gone loopy-loo!
He wears a tartan bow tie
And worst of all
He thinks his cage is a TARDIS
And goes, "Woo, woo, woo!"
Every time he gets in it for bed!

Marley Biney
Partney CE (A) Primary School, Partney

My Cat

My big long cat likes to go for walks
He is tall and fast with a stripy bow tie
He has a long tail and very big eyes
And very loyal big ears and very long arms
He is very vicious!
In the dark his eyes glow up like beams.

Toby Sutton (10)
Partney CE (A) Primary School, Partney

Jeff

My animal is big and brown
And looks like a real clown
He's got big black wings
And when he showers he will sing
My pet is the funniest thing
He eats black cheese - ming!
And wears bling!

Oscar Warren (10)
Partney CE (A) Primary School, Partney

The Cow

My cow is not like a lot of cows in the world
It's a sausage roll thief!
It eats all my sausage rolls
And gobbles them all up
When I go for a bite
All I get is straw!

Adam Middleton (10)
Partney CE (A) Primary School, Partney

Brownie The Dog

My cute brown dog has beautiful broad eyes
Huge shaggy ears
A long red tongue
Brown, miniature, fluffy feet
When I get home he likes to snuggle with me!

Gracie Stroud (10)
Partney CE (A) Primary School, Partney

Daisy The Dainty Dalicorn

The other day I was walking on the grass,
I saw an unusual Labrador that I seemed to pass,
At night I returned to see this creature again,
Then I came across her, she was very contained,
She spread her wings and grew a unicorn horn,
She flew up into the sky and landed on my lawn!
Sparkle, sparkle, sparkle!

I took her home and gave her a bath,
Then I dried her off and took her down the path,
She spread her wings that sparkled,
And grew a unicorn horn,
I wonder what she will do next?
I bet I would be startled,
She put me on her giant back and we flew away,
But first we made sure the house was okay on this crazy day!
Sparkle, sparkle, sparkle!

Daisy the Dalicorn is a peculiar pet,
She is the craziest pet I have ever met!

Harriet Jones (9)
St Mary's Catholic Primary School, Little Crosby

A Dancing Melody

I once had a kitten
And she did something rather strange
So settle down and listen up or you just might get bitten
And if you're a dog person, well that might just change.

So my cat Melody was very charming
After all, she was a calico cat
Ballet was Melody's talent, though I'm no good that's for sure, all I know is farming
And she was definitely not your cat-that-sits-on-the-mat

She would dance around the room
And she would jump and twirl and spin
She had so much balance she could even dance with her nose holding a spoon
I entered her in competitions and she would always win!

I love this peculiar pet of mine
Though she takes up all of my time!

Molly Tarpey (10)
St Mary's Catholic Primary School, Little Crosby

Roko The Rock Bunny

Yesterday I bought a bunny
She was sweet, cuddly and funny
When night came she disappeared
I did not think much of it, it was a little weird
Next, she was performing at a rock concert
1, 2, 3, 4, rock and roll could be heard
This bunny was not right
She was actually giving me a fright
Carrots fell from the sky
As she yelled, "Hello Bunnyville!"
It could be heard from every hill
Then she pulled out a guitar and stood still
Roko the bunny played a nice song
Although it did not last long
All the bunnies looked drunk
One was dressed like a chipmunk

Roko the bunny was a peculiar pet
I am glad we met!

Elsie Croxton (9)
St Mary's Catholic Primary School, Little Crosby

Charlie The Nerd Bunny

Yesterday I saw a bunny
He was wearing glasses
It was oddly funny
Then I saw him hold a book
So I went to take a look

Not long after, he fell into a pool
But he backflipped out and it looked quite cool
I found a tag clipped on his tuxedo
That said: 'My name's Charlie'
But what surprised me the most
Was when he said, "That pool looks very gnarly!"

Hearing the sound of his voice
I wanted to ask him
But I had no other choice
I went to ask him but I couldn't even try
He got a jet pack and flew up into the sky

This is the most peculiar kind
That anyone could ever find!

Stevie-Leigh Connaughton (10)
St Mary's Catholic Primary School, Little Crosby

Duncan The Dancing Doggy

The other day I was walking along
Until I heard a peculiar song
Flashing lights was all I could see
So I got a little closer to see who it could be
I finally realised who it was...

It was Duncan the dancing doggy!

He was shining like a star to all of the crowd
They were cheering and shouting very loud
But who wouldn't love a dog like that?

It was Duncan the dancing doggy!

He was the coolest guy in town
Always jigging and dancing and spinning around
He was awfully rich
He had a million pounds
He was better than a goldfish, a tortoise or a moggy.

It was Duncan the dancing doggy!

Grace Hayes (9)
St Mary's Catholic Primary School, Little Crosby

Lucy The Adorable Lion Cub

Yesterday I found a lion cub
She loved to dress up
She had a cute cup
And wore lots of make-up
Roar, roar, roar.
A big yellow cat
She suddenly started chasing a mouse
Wearing a small hat
She was near my house
Roar, roar, roar.
I gave her food
She had a drink
Suddenly she's in a mood
Then had a think
Roar, roar, roar.
She went to bed
And her head
Popped with ideas

She will go out tonight
Roar, roar, roar.
I made her bed
And she loved it
It was pink and red
She loved to knit
Roar, roar, roar.
Lucy the adorable lion cub
That I will never forget!

Lucy Bovill (9)
St Mary's Catholic Primary School, Little Crosby

The Most Craziest Night Ever!

The other day I spotted a sloth,
He started to sing,
But then all of a sudden he started to cough,
Then he ate a moth.

It was really funny
But the sloth just wanted money
At this point I felt really sorry
So I gave him some money.

He was so grateful he gave me a show
Which was so funny
When it ended it was 12:49am
Which gave me a fright
Soon it would be light.

This night was so cool
I'm going to tell everyone at school.

Spotty the sloth was so cool, he was a strange pet
But he is the best pet I ever met!

Liam Yates (10)
St Mary's Catholic Primary School, Little Crosby

Dino-Fisha-Duck

The other day after school I was waiting for my dad
I waited and waited
Until something so strange leapt out of a bush, I nearly fainted!
It was a dino and ducky and fishy
And his back end was a little squishy
His face was a little round
But something about him made my heart pound
This thing was jumping through fire
When it said, "I can do a backflip." I said, "Liar!"
Then in my head a bulb turned on
"Come to the circus, you'll be number one!"
After that he gave me luck
Silly old dino-fisha-duck!

Eleanor Arthur
St Mary's Catholic Primary School, Little Crosby

Electric Elephant

Hi, I'm Ethan
And I'm scared to be eaten
I am so dumb
I swallow my gum.

Dumb, dumb, dumb!

His name is Billy
He is so silly
He is my friend
Who's round the bend!

Silly silly Billy!

I'm very cool
Cos I have a pool
I hang out all day
With my bae

Cool cool pool!

Hi I'm Ethan
And I'm scared to be eaten
Why am I repeating this?

Come closer and I'll give you a kiss!

Electric Elephant is a creepy kind
This poem is all in his mind!

Caleb Still (10)
St Mary's Catholic Primary School, Little Crosby

Brat The Cat

Pets, pets
Free money for the vets
This one's worst enemy is the wet
Well no, it's Super Sausage dropping sausages on his head
He really wishes he would be dead

Hiss, hiss, hiss!

But today Brat had a plan
He would bribe him with a can
As he came to his hideout
All of a sudden he began to shout
Super Sausage came over to help
But he got caught in a net so started to yelp

Hiss, hiss, hiss!

Brat the cat is a peculiar pet
The best one I have ever met!

Nathan Hughes
St Mary's Catholic Primary School, Little Crosby

Ballerina Bear!

This is my ballerina bear,
She has a pink tutu she loves to wear.
She spins and she flips,
She does millions of fancy tricks.

But that's on her good days...

She twirls and she falls,
She crashes into walls.
She is always stumbling,
But she is good at tumbling!

She tries her best,
But never rests.

This is my ballerina bear,
She has a pink tutu she loves to wear.
This is my peculiar pet,
I will not ever forget the first day we met!

Margot Buckley (10)
St Mary's Catholic Primary School, Little Crosby

Amy The Uni-Deer

One day I went on a walk
One day I went on a walk
My eyes caught on this creature
It was like a new rainbow feature

Next she vomited out a rainbow
At her enemy the crow
Then she just stood on the grass
I thought that was the last

Then I heard a sound
It was echoing all around
She whispered her name
"Amy," she also had a beautiful mane

Amy the Uni-deer was a peculiar pet
She was the craziest one I had ever met!

Zoe Hill (9)
St Mary's Catholic Primary School, Little Crosby

Rainbow Bunnycorn

The other day I saw a bunny
She was jumpy, beautiful and funny
She had big rainbow wings
And her horn was a wonderful thing
It was so sparkly it made my eyes shine
I couldn't believe Bunnycorn was mine
First she got up and did a funny dance
It looked like she was wearing clown pants
She was on the way to blush herself up
When she suddenly fell over the cup

Rainbow Bunnycorn is rather mad
If she left me I would be rather sad.

Isabella Williams (9)
St Mary's Catholic Primary School, Little Crosby

The Amazing Lotty And Henry

The other day I met a dog
It was very fluffy
Nothing like a bog brown log
And certainly not scruffy
Woof, woof, woof.
A day later I saw it again
And this time she had a friend
I called them Lotty and Harry
But all of a sudden Lotty started to dance
Woof, woof, woof.
Lotty and Harry are the most peculiar pets
One of a kind and the best of their kind
Now me and Lotty dance the night away in the garden!

Lauren Clegg (9)
St Mary's Catholic Primary School, Little Crosby

Lucky Ducky

Last night I was walking round the park
And I spotted a ducky
He seemed pretty lucky
Quack, quack, quack.

I took him home and gave him a bath
Then dried him off and took him down the path
Quack, quack, quack.

My ducky duck was one of a kind
He had the craziest, silliest mind
Sometimes he would float in the sky
And he would spread his beautiful wings and fly.

Angel-Rose Banner (10)
St Mary's Catholic Primary School, Little Crosby

The Classroom Mouse

The other day I spotted an ordinary mouse
That lived in an ordinary house
But she was a teacher
And by the way I said teacher not preacher.

This little mouse will be your furry friend for life
She never causes any strife
This mouse is very smart
And has a big loving heart.

This little mouse is one peculiar pet
Definitely one of the weirdest I've ever met!

Angelica Moffett (10)
St Mary's Catholic Primary School, Little Crosby

Fancy Flamingo

This is my fancy flamingo
She is very unusual
Because she likes to play bingo
She's always winning but never brags
Without a doubt
She's got this in the bag.

She goes by the name Little Miss Foe
She is very adorable
Because she has a red bow.

This is my fancy flamingo
She is one of a kind
The most peculiar pet you will ever find!

Emily West (10)
St Mary's Catholic Primary School, Little Crosby

The Day My Tiny Turtle Went Faster Than Sonic!

The other day I went in the sea
I saw a turtle so I decided to take it home with me
I bought a swimming pool so that he could swim around
It was the cutest I had found
I named him Tiny the turtle
He flipped around and swam finely
He could move faster than a car
He was like a rocket flying far
Tiny the turtle is the best pet
Better than all the rest!

Callum Clegg (10)
St Mary's Catholic Primary School, Little Crosby

The Rainbowcat

One day I bought a cat
She was lying on a mat
When it turned night
She went on a flight
And all you could see
Was Rainbowcat on the mat.

Hair fluffy like a bear
Fur darker than the night
Eyes as blue as the sea so shiny and bright
I knew my cat was different from the rest
But that doesn't bother me
Rainbowcat's the best!

Matthew Cunliffe-Davies (9)
St Mary's Catholic Primary School, Little Crosby

My Funky Monkey

Today I saw a monkey
He looked very funky
He had a shiny crown
And his fur was all brown
He had a bright red bow
And his name was Big Man Joe

He ate bananas
In his pyjamas
And he watched telly
With his tubby belly

Big Man Joe was very cool
He was the most peculiar pet I will ever know.

Lucy Bromilow (10)
St Mary's Catholic Primary School, Little Crosby

Funky Fish

The other day I spotted a fish
He was cute and quite smallish
He was extremely colourful and a little gullible

He thought he was a good writer
Always a strong fighter
And he swam against the tide
He never tried to hide

Funky Fish is a peculiar pet
The best I've ever met.

Summer Aldridge (10)
St Mary's Catholic Primary School, Little Crosby

Oh Crocko Naldo!

I went to see the cup finals
You'll never guess what I saw?
The greatest scorer of all time

Oh Crocko Naldo!

I heard he was a cup winner
The best they'd ever seen
He dribbles past the players
And scares the other team

Oh Crocko Naldo!

They say he has three legs
They say he has sharp claws
He tackles all the players
And scores the winning goals

Oh Crocko Naldo!

He nutmegs all the players
They seem to run and hide
For every time he scores a goal
They all have such a fright

Oh Crocko Naldo!

The crowd were screaming and chanting
But I couldn't see a thing
Oops, silly me, put my glasses on
And had a look to see
The greatest footballer was a crocodile
Who'd eaten up the team!

Oh Crocko Naldo!

Fahd Patel (10)
St Pius X Catholic Preparatory School, Fulwood

Basilafinshark

B asilafinshark looks big but is a gentle algae eater
A thing so ferocious and vicious is not expected to be a good swimmer
S o smart, so big, so fast, but somehow he has four tails
I nside the big blue sea he never enjoys reading books
L oving the size of his 58 metres and 385 tons
A mazing as he loves to eat buns
F unny when it comes to jokes about fish
I t will be hilarious before he is finished
N ot so small when you hear its sound
S marter than me is thought to be bound
H airy as an alpaca with seven huge fins
A s committed as her as he tips over tins
R ipping the seabed
K icking the coral with is body the colour red.

Abdullah Hussein (9)
St Pius X Catholic Preparatory School, Fulwood

Numsey The Ostrich

This is the tale of my ostrich named Numsey
He is ever so clumsy
He has a fascination with the moon
He keeps on saying, "I'm going in June"
One day he saw a poster on the wall
"Fly to the moon from Beijing" was the call
He ran incredibly fast back home
Tripping over his garden gnome!
He packed his bags in a hurry
And off he went in a scurry
He got his ticket and hopped on the train
Which was whistling its way off to Spain
He arrived at Barcelona, not Beijing
He jumped off scratching his head with his wing
Oh dear my feathery Numsey
You really are so clumsy!

Aamina Ali (9)
St Pius X Catholic Preparatory School, Fulwood

Chamelitten

Chamelitten is a wonderful pet
A mixture of chameleon and kitten.
It's cute and adorable with colourful fur
And is usually found in Great Britain.

It has an amazing ability to climb high trees
Its favourite food is cheese,
Which it likes served with fish and peas.

I love Chamelitten, my wonderful pet,
It's cute like a rainbow among the trees
And changes colour in the breeze.

Beatrice Constable (8)
St Pius X Catholic Preparatory School, Fulwood

Dr Falpd

F erocious flames coming out of his tail
A mazing animal, but not to keep as a pet
L azy animal, it just eats leftovers like a hyena
P urple fur, very soft, but when you touch it you will get an electric shock
D r Falpd is always moaning to go to work. Just don't go near it and you will be safe!

Aayush Patel (8)
St Pius X Catholic Preparatory School, Fulwood

Rex, My Cat

R ex is a clever cat
E gg is his favourite
X ylophone is his favourite instrument

M og is Rex's best friend
Y eah! Rex is the best cat ever!

C urly hair, very fair
A crobatics is his favourite workout
T hat is the end of Rex, My Cat.

Faheem Patel (8)
St Pius X Catholic Preparatory School, Fulwood

Jagilla

J ane has gorilla arms and jaguar legs
A jagilla is great!
G reat speed, as fast as a wild beast and strong! *Whoosh! Roar!*
I nteresting scales and stealthy
L ength is 35 metres
L arge arms that are 90 cm
A nd fast legs!

Gerard Ologbosere (8)
St Pius X Catholic Preparatory School, Fulwood

The Intelligent Tiger

Have you ever heard of an educated tiger?
Or a tiger that goes to school?
My tiger does
He learns more and more each day
His favourite subject is PE
He always wins the race
He's learned about algebra and graphs in maths
He's such an intelligent tiger!

Hashim Syed Shoab
St Pius X Catholic Preparatory School, Fulwood

The Tiphant

My pet is a tiphant
He loves playing football
He scores a lot of goals in football
He is really thin
He can also run really fast
He can tackle opponents
He can't be stopped, he just keeps going
My tiphant is the best animal to have in the world!

Zain Ahmad (9)
St Pius X Catholic Preparatory School, Fulwood

Penpand

P ecky Fluffy is its name
E xcited wherever it goes
N icer than anything in the world
P rotective to its owner
A dorable than ever
N ever ever dangerous
D umber than anything you can imagine.

Keean Taherian (9)
St Pius X Catholic Preparatory School, Fulwood

Speedy Sloth

My sloth is very speedy
He races to the shops
He likes to play with all his friends
And eats blue lollipops.

He cuddles me at night-time
And stays there all night long
As soon as the alarm goes
He moans and groans a lot!

Sophie Fitzherbert (9)
St Pius X Catholic Preparatory School, Fulwood

Flash The Sloth

My sloth is a photographer
But he always falls asleep
He asks his friends to stand in line
Zzzz... he's gone again!
Wake up sloth!
Oh sorry, what day is it?
Never mind Flash, just go back to sleep!

Amelia Kovvuri (9)
St Pius X Catholic Preparatory School, Fulwood

YOUNG wRITERS INFORMATION

We hope you have enjoyed reading this book – and that you will continue to in the coming years.

If you're a young writer who enjoys reading and creative writing, or the parent of an enthusiastic poet or story writer, do visit our website **www.youngwriters.co.uk**. Here you will find free competitions, workshops and games, as well as recommended reads, a poetry glossary and our blog. There's lots to keep budding writers motivated to write!

If you would like to order further copies of this book, or any of our other titles, then please give us a call or order via your online account.

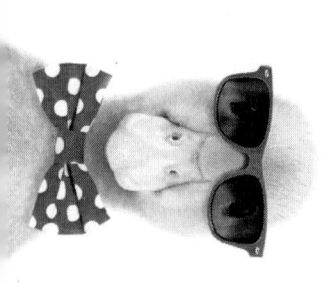

Young Writers
Remus House
Coltsfoot Drive
Peterborough
PE2 9BF
(01733) 890066
info@youngwriters.co.uk

Join in the conversation!
Tips, news, giveaways and much more!

YoungWritersUK   @YoungWritersCW